Ulrich Hub

ONE WISE SHEEP

—— *Based on a true story* ——

Illustrated by Jörg Mühle

Translated by Helena Kirkby

GECKO PRESS

Our story takes place one dreary winter around 4 BCE under the rule of a malevolent king who doesn't appear in this book. That's because he spends the whole time hiding in the attic of his palace, afraid that another king will come along and snatch his crown. Instead, there are sheep in this story. Lots of them. A sheep with its wool parted on the side, a sheep with its leg in a cast, a sheep who had braces and now wears a retainer, and many more. Only the shepherds know exactly how many. They count their flock several times a day. Their job takes nerves of steel. Not a single sheep may be lost.

Not even the last sheep.

People tend to think that sheep just stand

peaceably in fields munching contentedly on grass. But really, they spend the whole time running around and making a racket. As soon as one sets off, the next follows, in case they've found something interesting to eat. Sheep are all out for themselves, and it's always the same ones who kick and shove or simply trample over the others.

Only once night falls does silence suddenly descend. No sheep would ever admit to being afraid of the dark but, to be on the safe side, they snuggle together and try to fall asleep as quickly as they can. Usually, they sleep through the night.

Tonight, though, everything is different.

CHAPTER 1

The whole field is lit up, as if by a gigantic floodlight. Every rock, every thistle and every nibbled blade of grass can be clearly seen.

All the sheep are awake and staring open-mouthed at the night sky. A new star is up there, shining as bright as dawn. It can't be a good sign. Someone should check it out with the shepherds.

"The shepherds have gone!" comes a distant cry, from the sheep with the snuffly nose. The others make the sheep with the snuffly nose sleep away from the rest of the flock—none of them want to catch something. "Gone! Vanished!"

Nothing like this has ever happened before. Shepherds abide in the fields; they have to stay with their sheep at night. If a sheep suddenly wakes up from a bad dream—about the big bad wolf, say—it only has to trot over to the shepherds crouched around their little fire. Then they take the frightened sheep in their arms, comfort it and carry it gently back to the flock. But only once it has fallen back to sleep.

The sheep race to the fire. What they see is a picture of horror: the coals are cold, a feeble trail of smoke hangs in the air, and the shepherds have vanished without trace.

Only their backpacks remain lying on the grass.

"Well, this is a fine pickle," says the last sheep to arrive, who considers itself the brains of the flock. "Now we're on our own. It's going to be a disaster."

The sheep with the side part immediately starts crying. "Our shepherds left because they don't love us anymore! They always said it would be easier to herd a bag of fleas than sheep like us!" Big tears roll from its eyes. "They've gone to find better-behaved animals. A herd of cows or goats or even geese."

Nobody ever cries in front of the whole flock! The sheep exchange glances. But then, the whole side-part business is already embarrassing. This sheep is the only one to be combed by the shepherds each morning. The others have long since kept their fleeces to themselves.

There's a sudden crackling and rustling. The sheep flinch. But it's just the sheep with the plaster cast, limping nimbly from one backpack to the next, poking its nose into each.

"Only spare socks and toothbrushes," it mutters. "You'd think they might have left a few treats in their backpacks."

All sheep are extremely greedy—eating is the thing they love best—but the others find the pack-rummaging a bit much. "Pull yourself together!" they cry indignantly. "That's theft! We'll be in big trouble when the shepherds come back."

"Don't worry, the shepherds won't be back." The sheep with the bobble hat laughs gruffly. "You were all fast asleep, but I watched the whole thing. Very carefully."

The others groan in annoyance.

Of *course* the sheep with the bobble hat claims to have seen something. That one's barmy. Always seeing things that aren't there—or haven't happened yet. It recently said that they'd have telephones and televisions in the future. Things no sheep has ever heard of and that sound completely unbelievable.

"I woke up in the middle of the night," the sheep with the bobble hat begins in a croaky voice. "At first, I felt a weird tingling and prickling all over my body. Then a huge, silent, glowing apparition floated down. Out of nowhere, this high voice started singing." The sheep rolls its eyes so only the whites can be seen. "Fear not: for, behold, I bring you good tidings!"

A shiver runs down the spines of the listening sheep.

"But our shepherds were very scared," the sheep with the bobble hat continues croakily. "And suddenly a host of angels appeared in our field singing praises. I think I even heard trumpets—"

"And the good tidings?" the others insist. "What were they?"

The sheep with the bobble hat thinks briefly. "I've forgotten."

"Concentrate! Tidings are always important!"

"Something about … waddling crows."

The others sigh loudly. "You're hopeless. What about the shepherds?"

"They were kidnapped."

"Kidnapped?"

"By the UFOs."

"UFOs?" The sheep are bewildered.

"Unidentified flying objects steered by aliens," the bobble-hat sheep whispers. "We are not alone."

UFOs: well, *they* actually sound reasonable. More so than televisions and telephones, anyway. Suddenly all the sheep feel a tingling and prickling.

What if the UFOs are about to return?

The flock blows a fuse. The sheep race wildly about the field, trying to hide behind rocks—until they remember what the shepherds have told them countless times: "Always stay together. Not a single sheep must be lost."

As if on command, they all sprint back and form again as a flock. As they have learned to do: each sheep ruthlessly shoves the others aside to reach the coveted spot in the middle, where it's safest.

Only the sheep with the snuffly nose has dashed away so fast from fear of the UFOs that it's reached the far edge of the field. It looks with curiosity at the line of odd stones evenly arranged on the ground.

This far and no further! The shepherds have said it countless times. But then, what haven't the shepherds said countless times?

The sheep steps boldly over the line, breath held.

Nothing happens.

Well, well.

It glances back. The others stand huddled in the field. Then it looks ahead and stiffens.

Between the branches of a small tree stands a shaggy figure—with yellow eyes, horns on its head, and a cloven hoof.

The sheep lets out a squeal, then at once feels ashamed of being afraid. A sheep need not be intimidated by a goat.

"How do you do," the sheep greets the goat. "Did you happen to notice anything out of the ordinary this evening?"

"Once again, you muttonheads are the last to get it." The goat has an attitude from the outset. "The winged messengers proclaimed the good tidings everywhere—"

"Hang on," said the sheep. "They weren't UFOs?"

The goat looks at the sheep as if it's lost its

mind. "UFOs? You sheep are even stupider than I thought. Do you want to know the good tidings or not?" Before the sheep can answer, the goat says in an important voice: "Today is a great feast day. And tomorrow will be a feast day too. The whole village is fired up. For unto us a child is born and you shall find it wrapped in swaddling clothes—"

"A baby!" the sheep snuffles.

"Stop interrupting," the goat snaps. "And blow

your nose. By the way, it's not just any old kid. The birth has been predicted for ages and everyone's been longing for the great moment, but the due date kept on being postponed. Then tonight at last it happened."

"What does the baby look like?"

While the sheep and the goat go on with their chat behind the tree, the flock is in uproar. Where's the sheep with the snuffly nose? Nobody's seen it for ages. They all sigh together.

"We're off to a great start," says the last sheep. "One lost already. Probably kidnapped by the UFO. At least none of us will catch that cold now."

"Atchoo!"

They hear a sneeze, then the familiar nasal voice. "Fear nod!"

They all turn round. The sheep with the snuffly nose is standing in full starlight, proclaiming: "I bring you good—"

But it gets no further, as accusations pour in from all sides. "You can't just come and go as you please. We were out of our minds with worry. You have to tell us if you're going somewhere. Especially since UFOs are constantly taking off and landing here."

"They weren't UFOs—they were winged messengers." The sheep huffs and sniffs. "Anyway, I know the tidings."

"Well, then." The sheep crowd closer. "Why didn't you say so? What are the tidings?"

"Too late. I'm not telling you." The sheep turns away from the flock. "The tidings are my secret."

"That's not fair! The tidings are all of our business. At least tell us if they're good tidings or bad."

"Good tidings. I'll say that much. The feast days began today. Huge changes are coming. You won't believe your eyes or ears."

"Too exciting!" The sheep bounce up and down like excited table tennis balls. "Tell us the good tidings! What are they?"

All at once, everyone wants to be friends with the sheep with the snuffly nose and seems not to mind catching a cold—but the sheep coolly rejects all friend requests.

Until the sheep with the retainer comes along

with an offer it can't refuse. "If you tell me the tidings," it lisps, "I'll lend you my retainer."

Everyone gasps. This sheep is the envy of the flock on account of the retainer. But the treasure is kept in a little box hung on a cord around its neck, and the sheep has never been willing to part from it even for a minute—always using the same excuse: "You'll end up breaking it."

Given the tempting prospect of finally being allowed to wear the coveted retainer, the sheep with the runny nose is happy to share the secret. The other sheep's ears are flapping like rhubarb leaves, so the two of them duck behind a rock and conspire in whispers.

"A baby was born unto us tonight," the sheep with the snuffly nose whispers. "We shall find it wrapped in swaddling clothes, lying in a manger. Give me that retainer."

"Is that it?" the other sheep lisps. "Weird message. Babies are always swaddled."

"It's not any old baby." The sheep sticks its nose in the air crossly. "When it grows up, it'll be the savior of the world. Now give me the retainer."

"How do you know this?"

"I got it firsthand. From a goat. Now just give me that pesky retainer!"

"Pah! Those tidings aren't worth a bean."

The sheep with the retainer turns away coldly, stalks back to the flock and trumpets the tidings— about the swaddling, the baby, the salvation of the

world. "Someone's had their hoof pulled by a goat." The sheep laughs at its own little joke and looks around expectantly. But there was one thing it hadn't counted on...

"A baby!" the whole herd bleats in delight. "Babies are so unbelievably cute. Those little hands with their tiny little fingers, and those darling little feet!" But the most important question is, of course: "Is it a boy or a girl?"

The sheep with the snuffly nose thinks for a moment. What did the goat say? "The baby has long eyelashes, gorgeous curly hair and doesn't cry at all."

"It's a girl!" The flock can't contain themselves now—they whoop and cheer and jostle about. They're all set to march straight off to the village to see the newborn baby. Even the sheep with the retainer is beside itself.

"Why didn't you say that in the first place?" it lisps. "Girls are so much smarter than boys!"

Only the sheep with the side part holds back. "We can't do that," it warns. "We'd better stay here until the shepherds return. When you're lost, you're always supposed to stay where someone last saw you."

They all roll their eyes. That sheep is a total wet blanket! On feast days, all kinds of things are allowed, and everything is up for grabs. The shepherds must have already been in the village for a while. What a surprise they'll get, seeing their sheep turn up after such a long hike.

"And it's even more exciting because it's getting dark," says the sheep with the eye patch. "We'll be doing our first ever night hike."

The sheep quickly line up in pairs. They each make a mental note of their partner, then they're ready to go. Of course, pocket knives and matches are not permitted on a hike, although the sheep with the eye patch says otherwise. Now they just have to do a final count.

Unfortunately, sheep are not mathematically inclined. They don't have fingers, either, to secretly count on. But they're presumed to be all present and correct. The most important thing about a hike is to leave on time.

Quickly, the flock sets off. The sheep with the side part is paired with the sheep with the retainer; the sheep with the cast has the sheep with the snuffly nose, and so on. The last sheep brings up the rear—it doesn't have to remember its partner because it doesn't have one.

"The newborn baby will have been dying for visitors like us," it murmurs. "The sick, the lame and the complete crackpots. I bet she can't wait to kiss the hooves of this bunch of losers."

CHAPTER 2

The star in the night sky glows gold and casts enough light for a thrilling night hike. From the hilltop, they can clearly make out the village with its tumbledown houses. The flock chatters happily as it trips along the stony path.

When the path steepens, the sheep enjoy the climb, and their chests expand. As usual on a hike, they all start singing cheerful songs—until the sheep with the bobble hat joins in.

"Why did you stop?" the sheep croaks, puzzled. "It was sounding so pure and lovely. Almost heavenly."

Pretty soon, a picnic area invites a welcome rest. Fortunately the sheep with the cast had found some snacks in one of the backpacks and thought to bring it along. And since what you put in your stomach no longer has to be carried uphill on your back, all the sheep crowd around the backpack, stick their noses inside, and in record time munch up the treats.

"Oh brilliant," says the last sheep as it snaffles the last treat. "We've hardly begun, and we've already eaten our provisions."

The sheep shrug their woolly shoulders. There's bound to be a delicious meal in the village, so they can fill up there. On feast days, everyone eats from morning till night. "I can just picture the dinner table," the sheep with the bobble hat says. "Pastries,

roast poultry and—" it adds triumphantly
"—sausages and mash!"

That'll make a change from limp blades of grass.
And be far healthier than sugary snacks! The sheep
jump up at once and race on, leaving their litter
behind. Someone else will pick it up.

Just around the next bend, the flock stops abruptly.
Ahead lies a deep, dark forest. In the pale light of
the star, the tree trunks look as if they've been
painted black. Only a narrow path leads between
the tall trees into total darkness. But the sheep have
to go this way if they want to reach the village in
time for the festivities. They all prick up their ears
and listen. Is that something rustling and snorting
in the undergrowth? There are sure to be wolves in
there!

The sheep start to tremble. Who'll go first?

One of the most important rules of hiking is:
The weakest in the herd always goes at the front.

As if on command, they all look at the sheep with the cast.

"What are you looking at me for?" it says crossly. "I only have one bad leg. And when it comes to the weakest in the flock, I can think of several candidates right away. The blind, for starters." The sheep looks around. "Where's the one with the eye patch?"

Nobody has seen it for a while.

They all sigh.

"Oh great," says the last sheep. "We've lost another one. Probably fallen into a hole. Who was its partner?"

The sheep with the eye patch is meanwhile engrossed in animated discussion with an ox who's snuffling around for food scraps at the side of the path.

"If you want to visit this fabled child, you're going in completely the wrong direction." The ox chews on something. "It wasn't born in the village but down in our valley. Right behind the scrapyard."

"But there are only a couple of sheds and stables there," the sheep muses. "We can't go there. The shepherds have always said so. There's no fresh drinking water, the streetlights don't work properly, and even the police avoid the area."

"A few shepherds are already there. Probably yours." The ox is still chewing. "And by the way, they don't exactly look as if they've stepped out of a fashion magazine."

"Our shepherds make their own clothes entirely from natural fibers," the sheep retorts. "But tell me about the baby. Why would it choose to be born somewhere so dismal?"

"None of us chose to live behind a scrapyard," the ox says between bites. "But at least we stick together down there."

"What are you actually eating?"

"No idea."

"It's some kind of packing material." The sheep narrows its one eye. "You can't eat that sort of thing. It's definitely not healthy."

"Whatever." The ox goes on calmly chewing. "What choice do I have? I can't get anywhere near my manger. There's a baby asleep on the hay."

Meanwhile, up on the edge of the forest, the sheep are in heated debate about who was the partner of the one with the eye patch. The sheep with the snuffly nose claims that the sheep with the cast was the sheep with the eye patch's partner, although the sheep with the cast has absolutely no recollection of this, but finally remembers that its partner was the sheep with the bobble hat, although this is not what the sheep with the bobble hat remembers, although it finally recalls that its partner was the sheep with the retainer, although… Gradually, it dawns on the sheep what their shepherds meant: it really is easier to mind a bag of fleas than a flock of sheep.

"Back! Back! We're going completely the wrong way!" The sheep with the eye patch comes racing up the hill. "The baby was born in a hut down in the valley. The parents aren't from here and couldn't find room anywhere in the town—" The sheep stops by the flock, panting heavily. "The father tried every single inn."

"But everything's always booked up at this time of year!" Even the sheep know that. "Why didn't the parents make a reservation?"

"I wondered that too. But if the baby is going to be the savior of the world, being born amongst the poorest of the poor is a good start. Maybe the good tidings are that money and riches aren't that important."

"Nice idea," the sheep with the bobble hat croaks hoarsely. "But I can't see it catching on."

"And while we're at it, we need to talk to our shepherds about their clothing. Wool isn't necessarily the thing nowadays." The sheep with the eye patch takes another deep breath. "Anyway, we know where she is, the baby girl wrapped in swaddling clothes and lying in a manger."

"What?" The sheep are stunned. "In a manger? Who puts a newborn baby in a feeding trough? We need to have serious words with those parents."

The whole company about-turns. The sheep look down into the valley. The scrapyard is easily seen, shown to advantage by the flattering light of the new star. The hut must be just behind it. Some of the flock groan. All that uphill climbing for nothing. Luckily, the sheep find a little short cut. They simply let themselves tumble down the slope and land in the valley in record time.

Once there, however, they find a river blocking their way. The water rushes past between rocks.

"So much for short cuts," the last sheep says. "We should have stayed on the marked path. Nobody ever listens to me."

Fortunately, though, sheep can swim. They have weekly swimming lessons which usually coincide with bath day. Every sheep's nightmare! Hence most of them find a way out of it—for the flimsiest of reasons. Today, however, there are no excuses. They all hold their noses and leap into the water.

The sheep squeal as they paddle through the ice-cold current. But in the middle of the river they suddenly stop and tread water with their little legs. Where's the sheep with the cast? Casts aren't supposed to get wet. They all heave a big sigh.

"This just gets better and better," gasps the last sheep. "That's another one down. Probably still up on the hill, calling desperately for help."

"I'm over here!"

A cheerful voice comes from the other bank. The sheep with the cast found a bridge just around the bend, with a railing too, so it simply walked over the water. Now it's sitting comfortably on a bench, grinning as the others wade through the water. "Too slow for me," it calls. "I'm going on ahead. See you at the scrapyard!"

Without waiting to hear what the others have to say, the sheep with the cast hobbles off and soon makes an interesting acquaintance right beside the scrapyard.

"Lucky you, meeting me."

Under the flickering streetlight is a donkey in a grey fur coat. "I saw the birth in the stable up close. It was anything but fun, I can tell you. But now there's a baby in the manger. I almost cried when

I saw it. It wouldn't stop smiling. Somehow, it took a shine to me."

"So why aren't you still with the baby?" the sheep asks.

"Sweetfleece, I need a break too." The donkey casually clamps a stalk between its teeth. "I'm the one who lugged the heavily pregnant mother all this way."

"No one should make a long journey when they're about to give birth," the sheep points out.

"The parents had no choice." The donkey shrugs. "They had to come here to be counted."

"What? People get counted as well?" The sheep's eyes widen. "I had no idea. But just between you and me, why's the little girl in a manger?"

The stalk almost falls from the donkey's mouth. "Clearly there's a lot you don't know. The child is—" It thinks for a moment. "You'd better come with me to the stable. Be prepared for a gigantic surprise."

"What kind of surprise?"

"You'll see." The donkey grins from ear to ear. "I'll make sure you get a good seat. With a direct view of the manger. It's starting to fill up in the stable. People are coming from all over. A couple of guys on camels just turned up in strangely shaped hats, bringing all kinds of gifts from the East. Gold, frankincense and marjoram—"

At these words, the sheep gives a start, whirls round and hobbles quickly back towards the river.

"Where are you going?" the donkey calls after the sheep. "Did I say something wrong, sweetfleece?"

Meanwhile, the sheep have reached the near bank and have gathered under the bridge to shake the water from their fleeces.

"We need a gift!" The sheep with the cast leans over the railing. "When you visit a new baby, you always bring a little something! Everyone else has brought gifts."

Gifts! Why haven't any sheep thought of this? Exhausted, they sit down in horseshoe formation and ponder this tricky assignment: "A child was born in a stable. Come up with a suitable gift and give reasons for your choice."

The sheep's brains speed up and stall simultaneously.

"I'll give the baby a wooden sword!" the sheep with the eye patch bleats. "Because—all children like playing with weapons. Girls, too." The sheep with the cast gives it a kick for not putting its hoof up before speaking. Anyway, a weapon is out of the question: that's one thing they can agree on. The baby must learn to assert itself without resorting to violence in case it makes enemies in later life.

Further suggestions are discussed.

A bib? Too unimaginative! Something home-made? No time for that! A necktie? But it's a girl! A cuddly toy; a cute stuffed lamb, perhaps?

That will just make it want a real animal later!
A gift card? Too impersonal!

"This gift business is getting stressful," the last sheep groans. "Let's just buy something and enclose the receipt. They can exchange it after the holiday."

But they all ignore this because a suggestion that meets with unanimous approval has made its way around the group. The retainer! Then the baby will grow up with nice teeth.

Hopefully no one in the flock has any objection.

But where is the sheep with the retainer?

Nobody's seen it for ages.

They all sigh together.

"Over there!" shouts the sheep with the eye patch. "Still in the water! It won't last much longer!"

Aghast, the flock watches as the sheep paddles frantically after the little box with the retainer. It's barely keeping its head above water. At last,

it grabs the box, but next moment is caught by
the current. It clings bleating to a rock, only to be
swept off into a deep whirlpool. The flock squeals.

Splash!

In a death-defying move, the sheep with the side
part has jumped into the river, paddled to the scene
of the accident and dived into the current.

To cheers from the rest of the flock, the limp
sheep is dragged to the safety of the shore.

"Someone else can do mouth-to-mouth
resuscitation." The sheep straightens its hair.
"Since I've already risked my life."

However, it seems to be too late for lifesaving measures. The sheep with the retainer lies lifelessly on the bank. The little box hangs from its neck; water runs from its drenched fleece; its chest neither rises nor falls.

It hasn't been this quiet in the flock for a long time. A while back, the sheep found a dead bird that had fallen from its nest, which the shepherds carefully laid on a soft bed of moss. That was bad enough, but this...

"Now we're in a pickle," the last sheep says. "We've lost the sheep with the retainer forever. That's not how I imagined the holiday would be."

The others nudge the lifeless sheep with their muzzles, but it doesn't move. "It's not fair!" Sobbing, they throw themselves on the sheep and drum on its chest. "You can't do this to us! Come on, get up! Do you hear?!"

And the impossible happens: the sheep with the retainer staggers straight to its feet, coughs once in embarrassment, and spits out a bit of river water—and a small fish.

"This is when we could do with a camera," the sheep with the bobble hat whispers. "It's a shame they haven't invented it yet. Nobody will believe this story later."

Laughing in relief, the flock cuddles and nuzzles the resurrected sheep from all sides.

"I knew it," says the last sheep. "The sheep with

the retainer wasn't dead at all. It just wanted
attention."

"Must you always have the last word?" the
others say, shaking their heads.

"Well, you explain what you thought would
make a good present for the baby. I can't wait to see
the reaction." The last sheep gives a short laugh.
"Our friend will probably jump right back in the
water."

"What gift?" The sheep with the retainer is curious. "Out with it! Don't keep me in suspense. Why are you all giving me that funny look?"

"Er—" They all exchange glances. "We'll explain along the way."

Time is running out. The star in the night sky has turned from gold to orange and will soon be red. The sheep make their way quickly up the embankment.

Only the last sheep hangs back, muttering to itself. "I've had enough. I couldn't care less about the tidings. The others can fall on their knees in front of the stupid baby—they believe all they're told, like little kids. They're even still afraid of the big bad wolf." It turns away. "I have more brains than the rest of them put together. I'm going back to the field. At least I'll have some peace and quiet."

CHAPTER 3

Grey-black clouds have closed in over the new star by the time the last sheep arrives, exhausted, at the familiar field. Everything is in deep darkness—just like all the other nights.

"This is what I've always wanted." The last sheep looks around. "I finally have the whole field to myself. I'm alone and free."

It trots past nibbled blades of grass, sniffs at a thistle and looks around at the scattered boulder piles. "There ought to be a good view from the highest," it thinks and bravely starts the climb.

Nimbly it leaps from ledge to ledge and, before you know it, is at the top. Standing tall on the rocky summit, the last sheep proudly surveys its kingdom.

Suddenly there's a ferocious growl.

The sheep looks down from the rock and freezes.

Far below, a big black wolf is circling the boulder. Two wolves! Both are staring up. Despite the dark, they are wearing mirrored sunglasses.

"What are you doing out here all alone at night?" one of the wolves asks.

The sheep says nothing.

"Why are you still up at this hour? You ought to be asleep by now."

The sheep still doesn't answer.

"Where are your shepherds?"

The sheep has to say something. "They're asleep."

"I see," snorts the wolf, staring up at the rock. "And where are your friends? Sheep always come in flocks."

"I have no friends," says the sheep.

"Come on down, little one. We'd like to have a word with you."

The sheep holds its breath and doesn't budge.

"Are you coming?" The wolf tries to climb the rock, but its sharp claws keep slipping on the smooth stone.

The second wolf speaks up. "There's no need to be afraid of us." It takes off the mirrored sunglasses, switches on a smile, and stares up with cold green eyes. "We just need a little bit of information. A baby was born tonight. No doubt you've heard about it." The wolf goes on in a surprisingly gentle voice. "In this country there's a mighty king, with a real crown. When he first saw the new star and heard of the birth, he was horrified. He did his utmost to find the child's whereabouts."

"Why?" the sheep asks.

"So that he can go and—ahem—" the wolf clears its throat, "pay homage to the child."

"Pay homage?" The sheep has never heard of this, but it doesn't sound like a good thing.

"My colleague and I thought," the wolf continues, "that we could take the baby straight to his magnificent palace."

Only now does the sheep see with horror that
the first wolf has sunk its teeth into a little bush in
the rock face and is clambering steadily up.

"This is the first I've heard of a newborn baby,"
the sheep stammers.

"You're lying." Paw by paw, the wolf climbs higher, snorting in excitement. "I can smell it."

"I don't know the child you're talking about!"

With a powerful leap, the wolf reaches the ledge directly below the sheep. It raises a paw with its sharp claws, ready to strike—

"You'll find her right behind the scrapyard!" the sheep cries. "She was born in a stable!"

"She?" The wolf pauses in bewilderment.

"A girl in swaddling clothes, lying in a manger!"

"What?" The wolf looks down. "A girl?" Then it loses its balance and falls backwards down the rock face.

With a powerful thud, it lands at the feet of its colleague, who looks down shaking its head. "Why did I listen to you? We're looking for a boy. I told you we were wasting our time in this stupid nowhere."

Now the sheep on the rock starts trembling.
It can't stop and is still shaking when the wolves
have long since disappeared over the horizon.

A cool, gentle rain falls from the sky.

Exhausted, the sheep closes its eyes.

"You really are the limit!" some voices exclaim.

"You can't just run off. Do you really think we won't
notice?"

The last sheep's eyes fly open. All the sheep are
gathered around the boulder. They are standing
between the puddles, with dripping wet fleeces.

"And what are you doing up there? You've lost
your mind. Come down right now. We want to visit
the baby."

"Haven't you been yet?" the last sheep
stammers.

"We couldn't go without you," the others cry.
"Not a single sheep may be lost. Get a move on!
We don't have all night!"

The last sheep has never been so happy. Its eyes fill with tears. Don't start crying now, it tells itself.

"You have no idea what I've been through," it says. "I've never felt so alone, and when the wolves turned up—"

"You can tell us later. We have to get our skates on. The first visitors already passed us on their way home. The baby is a sensation! It's said to perform miracles. It can read thoughts, turn water into raspberry juice, and even bend a fork—just by looking at it."

"You believe that nonsense?" the last sheep grimaces. "It's probably just a cheap trick."

"We'd rather see for ourselves. Now come on! Or do you need a written invitation?"

The last sheep peers cautiously down. "But what about the gift?"

"We came up with a great idea on our way here," the sheep with the retainer lisps. "Straight from the heart and very personal. We made up a song and learned it as we walked."

"It was actually my idea," the sheep with the bobble hat croaks. "We lull the little one to sleep with the magic of our music."

But the last sheep stubbornly shakes its head. What's wrong now? The others tap their hooves impatiently.

Finally it dawns on the sheep with the eye patch. "You're too scared to come down, aren't you?"

The last sheep bursts into tears. "It's too high. I don't even know how I got up here."

"Don't worry!" the others bleat. They huddle together as tight as they can below the rock. "Just jump. We'll catch you."

The last sheep swallows hard. Then it screws up its eyes, steps out into nothingness, and lets itself fall.

There's rushing in its ears.

The last sheep is flying—

But not for long.

It lands gently on its friends' woolly backs as if on a big soft pillow.

"Strange." It looks up at the rock. "It wasn't actually all that high."

Its landing has made the other sheep collapse in a muddled heap, and they struggle for some time to stagger to their feet.

"What are you waiting for now?" the last
sheep says. "Don't dawdle, otherwise we'll reach
the famous stable only to find that the newborn
baby has long since become a young woman.
With curly hair."

The star in the night sky no longer shines yellow,
but bright red. The sheep rush down into the valley
through mud and puddles. Their fleeces are
splattered, their hairdos completely undone. Even
the sheep with the side part looks like a broom
gone mad. "The baby won't care what we look like,"
it gasps. "Newborns see everything upside down
and backwards anyway."

On the bridge, the sheep come upon crowds of
visitors. They're all carrying balloons and wearing
bright t-shirts printed with images of a sweet-
looking baby boy with curly hair.

Puffing and panting, the sheep scamper past the
scrapyard until, utterly done in, they reach the

huts. They wander through a maze of dark alleys. All are lined by stalls with carelessly stapled sprigs of pine, selling roast almonds, toffee apples and gingerbread. The sheep ignore them in their haste. The streets are growing emptier by the minute. Where is that pesky stable?

The sheep slow beside a ticket booth, feeling helpless, then round a final corner and find themselves in an abandoned courtyard. Dripping lanterns hang from washing lines, deflated balloons limp over the ground, while disposable cups and stuck-together sausage wrappers swim in puddles. At the far end of the courtyard is a rickety wooden shack.

That must be the famous stable!

The sheep stumble down a couple of damp steps, shove their way through the door, and stop. Fuggy air hits them. It takes a while for their eyes to adjust to the dark. A few empty plates are lying around on the floor. Rainwater drips steadily through the roof into an overflowing bucket.

In the middle of the stable is a manger.

"Careful," the last sheep whispers. "We don't want to wake her."

As quietly as they can, the sheep creep up to the manger, peer gingerly over the edge and emit a small collective squeal.

The manger is empty.

Apart from a few bits of straw and a tiny sock.

The sheep are too late.

"It's all my fault," the last sheep says softly.

"I'll never forgive myself. You even rehearsed your lovely song for nothing."

"Never mind," the others murmur.

"What if you sing it anyway?" The last sheep looks around sheepishly. "The baby might hear you anyway, wherever it is. It's supposed to have amazing abilities."

"You can sing along," the sheep with the retainer lisps. "The tune's very simple. It goes like this: Si-i-lent niiiight—"

The other sheep join in at once and sing from their hearts as they stand at the manger. The sheep with the bobble hat has the nicest voice: surprisingly high and clear.

As soon as the song ends, it starts croaking again. "Our song is sure to be a hit. People will still be singing it in a thousand years. All over the world. In different languages."

Meanwhile, day is dawning. The star in the night sky has vanished in the pale light of morning. With lowered heads, the sheep stumble out of the stable and bump into some strange animals who have settled on the ground in the middle of the courtyard.

"Mind where you're going. No need to stare so stupidly. Haven't you seen camels before?"

The sheep stammer out an apology.

"Let's take a wild guess." The camels yawn. "You wanted to see the newborn baby. Well, you clowns are a bit late."

"We've missed everything," the sheep groan. "How was it?"

"Terrible. Absolutely terrible!" The camels roll their eyes. "No wonder the kid's father had nightmares and secretly slipped away with his family. A ghastly brass band and inferior red wine—warm, as well." The camels shake their heavy heads. "People just lost it. They were all desperate to see the child. It was so packed that nobody could move. Whoever runs the local shop should have opened a second checkout counter."

"But the baby, the baby," the sheep persist. "Did you see it? Is it really that beautiful?"

The camels look at the sheep with slightly watery eyes. "We weren't stupid enough to wait in that queue. Everyone was only allowed a quick look in the manger anyway. Probably no one actually saw the boy with their own eyes."

"What? Boy?" The sheep are thunderstruck. "The baby isn't a girl? Are you sure?"

"Quite sure," the camels yawn. "Nobody makes that kind of fuss when a girl is born. Besides, the kid is supposed to save the world later. Girls are far too meek and mild for that."

"Hmm." The sheep have their own ideas on the topic. But they'd rather not get involved in discussion about it now. They have one more question.

A very important question.

"Can you, by any chance, count?"

"Come on!" The camels are indignant. "Mathematics was invented in Egypt. You can tell by looking at the pyramids."

"Then you'll be able to tell us how big our flock is. We've always wanted to know."

"We don't even need to count." Without moving their heads, the camels glance over the flock. "Seven."

"What?"

"Seven." The camels smile slightly. "How many did you think?"

"We thought there were at least a hundred of us!"

Camels aren't easily perturbed, but this is too much, even for them. "What a backwards country this is. And its inhabitants—entirely uneducated."

They stand abruptly, show the sheep their rear ends, and sway off. Maybe they drank a little too much of the lukewarm wine.

"We'd better get a move on and wake our people," they can be heard muttering. "Then get out of here. Back to the glorious East."

"Seven!" The sheep are devastated. As if things weren't bad enough. It turns out they're a meagre handful, they didn't see the baby, and they misunderstood the tidings. This holiday has been a litany of disasters.

The last sheep is the first to pipe up. "Well, we might have missed a big event but the whole world needn't know. If anyone asks what it was like in the famous stable, we can just say—" the sheep gazes with a rapturous look at the sky "—no words can describe it."

The others nod in approval and smile at the wise sheep. "If we get our stories straight, everyone will say: the sheep were there from the very beginning."

And together they rehearse that particular look with their eyes raised to Heaven.

The journey back to the field is calm and uneventful. The sheep do the right thing and pick up the litter they left at the rest stop. Only the sheep with the retainer amazes them all—by lending its retainer to the others without being asked. Every sheep is allowed to have a turn with it. A true act of charity.

When at last they reach the edge of their field, they barely recognize it. It's much smaller than they remember—and much lovelier. A kind of paradise. Tender green grass has grown up everywhere, following the gentle rain shower.

But what are those strange figures gathered around the fireplace? Tentatively, the sheep edge nearer, then stop in astonishment. It's the shepherds! In all the excitement, they had completely forgotten about the shepherds who abide in their field.

At the sight of the sheep, the shepherds jump up in joy and open their arms wide. And as the sheep come closer, they see that the shepherds have brought them something: roast almonds, shiny red toffee apples and gingerbread hearts.

Seven pieces.

One for each sheep.

"I told you so," the last sheep laughs. "This story has a happy ending."

"This story is far from over," the sheep with the bobble hat whispers. "It's only just begun."

This edition first published in 2024 by Gecko Press
An imprint of Lerner Publishing Group, Inc.
241 First Avenue North, Minneapolis, MN 55401 USA

English-language edition © Lerner Publishing Group 2024
Translation © Helena Kirkby 2024
Copyright text and illustrations
© 2018 by CARLSEN Verlag GmbH, Hamburg, Germany
First published in Germany under the title *Das letzte Schaf*

Gecko Press aims to publish with a low environmental impact. Our books are printed using
vegetable inks on FSC-certified paper from sustainably managed forests. We produce books
of high quality with sewn bindings and beautiful paper—made to be read over and over.

The translation of this book was supported
by a grant from the Goethe-Institut.

Original language: German
Edited by Penelope Todd
Typesetting by Katrina Duncan
Printed in China by Everbest Printing Co. Ltd,
an accredited ISO 14001 & FSC-certified printer

ISBN hardback: 9781776575954
ISBN paperback: 9781776575961
Ebook available

For more curiously good books, visit geckopress.com

Gecko Press publishes a curated list of children's books in translation from the best writers and illustrators in the world.

Gecko Press books celebrate unsameness. They encourage us to be thoughtful and inquisitive, and offer different—sometimes challenging, often funny—ways of seeing the world. They are printed on high-quality, sustainably sourced paper with stitched bindings so they can be read and re-read.

For more Gecko Press illustrated chapter books, visit our website or your local bookstore. You might like...

Duck's Backyard by Ulrich Hub and Jörg Mühle, in which an argumentative duck and a theatrical chicken go on a journey to a place where their dreams (might) come true.

Yours Sincerely, Giraffe by Megumi Iwasa and Jun Takabatake, for readers who like receiving letters and imagining things they've never seen.

Detective Gordon: The First Case by Ulf Nilsson and Gitte Spee, for detective stories set in a friendly forest, where Detective Gordon seeks justice for all and always makes time for delicious cakes.

A Bear Named Bjorn by Delphine Perret, for readers who enjoy a gentle bushwalk with an observant bear.